W9-BGW-072

My 1st Classic Story

Chicken Little

a retelling by Christianne C. Jones

illustrated by Kyle Hermanson

PICTURE WINDOW BOOKS
a capstone imprint

My First Classic Story is published by Picture Window Books
A Capstone Imprint
151 Good Counsel Drive, P.O. Box 669
Mankato, Minnesota 56002
www.capstonepub.com

Library of Congress Cataloging-in-Publication data
Jones, Christianne C.
Chicken Little / retold by Christianne C. Jones ;
illustrated by Kyle Hermanson.
p. cm. — (My first classic story)
Summary: When an acorn hits her on the head,
Chicken Little believes the sky is falling down and runs to
tell the king and everyone she meets along the way.
ISBN 978-1-4048-6072-8 (library binding)
[1. Folklore.] I. Hermanson, Kyle, ill. II. Title.
PZ8.1.J646Ch 2011
398.2—dc22
[E]   2010003619

Art Director: Kay Fraser
Graphic Designer: Emily Harris

The story of *Chicken Little* has
been passed down for generations.
There are many versions of the story.
The following tale is a retelling of the
original version. While the story has
been cut for length and level, the basic
elements of the classic tale remain.

One day, an acorn cracked Chicken Little on the head.

4

"Oh my!" she cried. "The sky is falling!
I must go tell the king."

Along the way, Chicken Little met Henny Penny.

"Where are you going in such a hurry?" asked Henny Penny.

"The sky is falling!" cried Chicken Little.
"We must go tell the king! Follow me!"

Soon they met Cocky Locky.

"Where are you two going in such a hurry?"
asked Cocky Locky.

"The sky is falling!" yelled Chicken Little.
"We must go tell the king! Follow us!"

Then they met Ducky Lucky.

"Where are you all going in such a hurry?"
asked Ducky Lucky.

"The sky is falling! We must go tell the king!"
yelled Chicken Little. "Follow us!"

Later they met Goosey Loosey.

"Where are you all going in such a hurry?" asked Goosey Loosey.

"The sky is falling! We must go tell the king!" cried Chicken Little. "Follow us!"

Then they met Turkey Lurkey.

"Where are you all going in such a hurry?" asked Turkey Lurkey.

"The sky is falling! We must go tell the king!"
yelled Chicken Little. "Follow us!"

So Chicken Little, Henny Penny, Cocky Locky, Ducky Lucky, Goosey Loosey, and Turkey Lurkey hurried off to tell the king the sky was falling.

They were well into their trip when they
met Foxy Loxy.

"Where are you all going in such a hurry?" snarled Foxy Loxy.

They all cried, "The sky is falling! We must go tell the king!"

"Oh no! You are headed in the wrong direction," said Foxy Loxy. "Follow me. I'll show you the way."

Chicken Little, Henny Penny, Cocky Locky, Ducky Lucky, Goosey Loosey, and Turkey Lurkey followed Foxy Loxy deep into the forest.

In fact, they followed Foxy Loxy
right into his cave!

Chicken Little, Henny Penny, Cocky
Locky, Ducky Lucky, Goosey Loosey,
and Turkey Lurkey have been missing
since that day.

And the king never did hear that the sky was falling.

31

The End